Co

Introduction

Charlotte Brontë

The Reverend Patrick Brontë, the clergyman in charge of the church at Haworth in Yorkshire, had six children. Five were girls. The four oldest girls were sent to a school for the daughters of clergymen at Cowan Bridge. Their mother had died, and their father did not know that the school was in an unhealthy place. It was badly managed, the girls did not get enough food, and the food was often bad. Some of the teachers were very unkind. Maria and Elizabeth, the two oldest sisters, died there in 1825. Charlotte, aged nine, and Emily, aged seven, were taken away from the school. Their aunt, who had come from Cornwall to look after the house at Haworth, gave Charlotte, Emily, and their youngest sister, Anne, their lessons after that.

Haworth was a lonely place for the clergyman's daughters. They were not allowed to play with the village children, and so they became even closer as a family. Like the Rivers' house in this story, their house was near but not in the village. From its windows they saw the graves beside the church, and beyond them the wild, almost treeless hill country of the Yorkshire moors. In winter the moors were cold and windy, so the Brontë sisters and their brother Branwell invented games to play in the house.

A game with Branwell's toy soldiers became a story about two rival nations. The children – all of them – began to write books about their nations. They were very small home-made books, some of them only 3.8 × 3.2 centimetres, with tiny imitation print. As the children grew older, they began to include poetry in their stories.

When she was fifteen, Charlotte became the teacher for Emily and Anne. In 1842, she and Emily went to Brussels (their aunt provided the money) to improve their knowledge of French. That visit came to an end when their aunt died later in the same year. Anne found work as a governess; Charlotte and Emily planned to open their own school. Meanwhile, all three of the sisters were writing.

At first it was poetry, and in 1846 they paid to have a book of *Poems* printed. There were poems in it by each of the sisters. The best of them were Emily's. The sisters called themselves Currer, Ellis and Acton Bell because they believed that women writers were not respected. By the time *Poems* was published, they were each at work on a novel. Emily's and Anne's novels were published first, both in 1847. Emily's *Wuthering Heights* is still read, and it is considered by many people to be one of the greatest tragic novels in English literature.

Charlotte's first novel, *The Professor*, did not find a publisher. But she also finished *Jane Eyre* in the same year, and it was published in October 1847. The writer's name was given as Currer Bell. The book was immediately popular. Currer Bell was famous.

By the middle of 1849, Charlotte Brontë, just thirty-three years old, was the only one of her father's six children still alive. Branwell, Emily and Anne were all dead. Charlotte had to look after her father, but she still found time to write two more novels, *Shirley* and *Villette*.

She married the Reverend Arthur Nicholls in June 1854 and became a busy and happy wife – for a few months. In March 1855, she was expecting her first child when a sudden illness took her life.

Jane Eyre

Nineteenth-century houses had better lamps than the houses of earlier times. A few homes even had gas lighting. The result was an increase in novel reading as a way of passing the long winter evenings. There was, of course, no radio, television or recorded music.

So, in 1847, when Charlotte Brontë's *Jane Eyre* was published, there was a large public eager to read good novels. Fielding had shown the way in the eighteenth century, and now in the nineteenth century Scott and Jane Austen had developed the form. Dickens had published *Oliver Twist*, *Nicholas Nickleby* and *The Old Curiosity Shop*. Thackeray's early work had appeared, but his great novel *Vanity Fair* (1848) was not yet published. Mrs Gaskell was about the same age as Charlotte Brontë but her *Mary Barton* came out in 1848, and *Cranford* in 1853.

Charlotte and Mrs Gaskell became friends, and it was Mrs Gaskell who wrote the life-story of Charlotte in 1857. That is how we know that Lowood in *Jane Eyre* was very much like the terrible school Charlotte attended.

What was – and is – important about *Jane Eyre*? It showed, as no novel before it had ever shown, a true understanding of human character and the causes of human behaviour. One thing Charlotte Brontë showed was that the inner nature of characters in a novel is more important than their appearance. What we remember about Jane Eyre is not her looks. It is her determined honesty, her common sense, and her goodness. Before *Jane Eyre*, the heroine of a novel had to be beautiful, or at least (like some of Jane Austen's heroines) attractive. Charlotte Brontë chose to make her heroine, Jane Eyre, plain, small and unattractive: "No one thought she was pretty, but Mr Rochester fell in love with her" (page 62).

Chapter 1
The Reed family

It was winter. The weather was very cold and it was raining. We could not go outside. I was glad; I never liked walks with my cousins, John, Eliza and Georgiana Reed. I was not a strong child. I always got tired before they did and then they laughed at me.

I did not like my cousins or my aunt, their mother. They did not like me, either. They never let me play in their games. I was very lonely at Gateshead Hall. But I had to live there because I was an orphan: my mother and father had died when I was a baby.

On that cold winter afternoon my cousins were sitting with their mother in the sitting room. My aunt did not allow me to be with them. I went to sit in the library. Reading was one of my greatest pleasures. The books in the library were not children's books, but I loved them.

Suddenly, the door opened and John Reed walked in. Eliza and Georgiana were following him.

"Where are you?" he shouted. "What are you doing? Come here at once!"

I stood up slowly. I was very frightened because John Reed was a big boy. He was fourteen years old and I was only ten. He was tall and very fat, because he ate too much. He was his mother's favourite. In her eyes he did nothing wrong. Suddenly he hit me so hard that I almost fell.

"What were you doing?" he shouted.

"I was reading," I answered quietly.

"Were you reading one of my mother's books?"

"Yes," I replied, and gave him the book.

"You mustn't read our family's books," he said. "You're

an orphan; your mother and father are dead; you have no money; you live with us because you have no other family. But you aren't one of our family and we don't like you." He lifted the book and hit my head with it.

For the first time in my life I showed that I was angry. All the unhappiness and loneliness of my life at Gateshead Hall came out.

"Wicked boy!" I cried.

John Reed was very surprised. "What did you say?" he shouted. "Did you hear that, Eliza and Georgiana? I'm going to the sitting room immediately. I'm going to tell Mother about you." Again he came towards me. He was going to hit me again. But this time I was ready, and I hit him first. I had never fought with him before. I pulled his hair and shouted, "You wicked boy! I hate you!" Mrs Reed and Bessie, one of the servants, appeared and pulled me away from my cousin.

"Take her to the red room and lock the door," my aunt said coldly.

"Take her to the red room!" Mrs Reed's words filled me with fear.

Bessie took me to it and locked the door. I looked round the room. It was a bedroom, but no one ever slept there now. My uncle had died there nine years before. Only the servants came here now. I sat where Bessie had left me. I was too frightened to move. I remembered Bessie's stories about ghosts. She said dead people often returned to their homes, especially if they were unhappy. I thought about the unhappiness and loneliness of my life with my aunt's family and I began to cry. My uncle had been kind to me while he was alive. Now no one loved me.

As the room grew darker, my fears grew too. I did not

Jane locked in the red room

dare to leave my chair. The noise of my heart grew louder and louder. I was terribly afraid. I cried out and ran to the door of the room. I heard Bessie outside.

"What's the matter? Are you ill?" she asked. She opened the door a little.

"Please, please, I must come out!" I cried. "I shall die in here."

"What's all this noise?" Mrs Reed's voice demanded.

"Jane cried out so loudly, Mrs Reed," Bessie answered, "that I thought she was ill."

"Take her back into the room. She must stay there for another hour," Mrs Reed cried angrily. "I have never seen a more wicked child."

"Oh aunt, please forgive me. I shall die in the red room," I cried.

"Be quiet," she shouted, and she pushed me back into the room.

After that I remember only darkness.

I woke up much later in my own bed. Someone lifted me carefully. I felt very strange. I heard voices, but they were a thousand miles away. Slowly, I began to see more clearly. Bessie was in the room, and Dr Lloyd.

I knew he was a kind man, and I was glad when he sat down by my bed. He began to ask me questions. I listened carefully and I answered easily. After a time Dr Lloyd said, "Well, Jane, I think you'll be better soon. I must go now, but I'll come back tomorrow. Bessie, the child must sleep now. Goodbye to you both."

For a time I felt happier. Bessie spoke kindly to me and this was unusual. But the sadness remained. I asked Bessie why I was in bed.

"You're ill because you were so frightened in the red

room. Now, be a good girl and try to sleep."

The next day Bessie dressed me and I got up. I felt very weak and sad. Bessie was still very kind to me. But nothing stopped the sadness in my heart. I cried a lot.

Dr Lloyd came to see me later in the day. He sent Bessie away.

Then I told Dr Lloyd about my troubles: about my loneliness at Gateshead Hall; about my aunt and cousins who hated me; about my sadness because I was an orphan. Dr Lloyd asked me if I had any other family. I replied that Mrs Reed had once told me about the Eyres. They were my father's family. She did not know where they lived. She said they were too poor to look after an orphan.

"Would you like to go to school?" Dr Lloyd asked me next.

"Yes, I think that I would like to go to school very much," I answered.

"Well," Dr Lloyd said, "I'll go and speak to your aunt about it. Goodbye, Jane."

Bessie told me later that my aunt had agreed with Dr Lloyd's idea. At the same time, Bessie told me about my mother and father. My father had been a poor clergyman. My mother's family, the Reeds, were very rich. They did not want her to marry a poor clergyman. They wanted her to marry someone rich and important. But she had married my father. Her family were very angry and they never spoke to her again. My father died a year later, just before I was born. Soon after, my mother died too.

"Poor Jane," said Bessie when she had finished. "It's a sad story. But you know, you must try to be more polite to your aunt's family. They've been very good to you."

Chapter 2
Lowood

One morning, almost four months later, Bessie came into my room.

"Mrs Reed wants you to go to the sitting room immediately," she said.

I was very frightened when she said this, but I had to go downstairs.

A very tall man, dressed in black, was standing in front of the fire in the sitting room. His face was serious and he did not smile once during the talk which followed.

He looked at me for a minute and then said, "She is very small. How old is she?"

"Ten, Mr Brocklehurst," my aunt replied.

"Really? She looks younger." Then he turned to me. "What is your name?"

"Jane Eyre, sir," I answered.

"And are you a good child?" he continued.

Here my aunt spoke: "Jane Eyre is a wicked child. I want her to go to your school at Lowood. I want her to grow up into a better person."

When Mrs Reed said this I hated her more than ever before. How could she talk about me like this? Especially to a stranger! Mr Brocklehurst would think of me as a wicked child for ever.

"Well, Mrs Reed," said Mr Brocklehurst, "I will tell Miss Temple, the head teacher of Lowood, that a new girl will be arriving soon. I shall also tell her what you have told me about this child."

And so my aunt's bad opinion of me went ahead of me to Lowood.

I left Gateshead very early in the morning. Only Bessie got up to say goodbye to me.

It was night when I arrived at Lowood, but I could just see a long, low building. I was taken into a sitting room. A tall, dark-haired woman with a kind face came in. When she saw me she said, "You must be Jane Eyre. You're very young to travel alone. Is this the first time that you have left your mother and father?"

I explained that I was an orphan. She asked me how old I was and then she said, "I hope you'll be a good girl at Lowood, Jane."

Then a teacher took me to have supper. We walked to a large room. It was full of girls of every age. There were about eighty of them, and they all wore ugly brown dresses and heavy shoes. Even the prettiest girls looked strange. They were learning their lessons for the next day.

Suddenly a voice said, "Bring the food for supper." But when the food arrived, I saw that there was only bread and water. There was so little that the meal ended very quickly. Then we went to bed.

I woke up the next morning when a bell rang. My life at Lowood School had really begun. We went down to the school room. There was one teacher for each of the four classes in the room. I was put in the lowest class. For an hour we had lessons, and then it was time for breakfast. I was so hungry that I was almost ill. But the smell of the food was so terrible that no one could eat very much.

We returned to our lessons until noon. Then we all went outside into the garden for half an hour. It was very cold and we had only very thin coats. Some of the girls coughed a lot; too many of them had weak chests.

I saw an older girl who was sitting alone. She was reading. For some reason I did not feel afraid of her. I dared to ask her some questions about the school. She answered kindly and explained that Lowood School was for orphans and children of poor families.

"Who is the lady I met yesterday evening?" I asked. "Does she own the school?"

"That's Miss Temple," was the answer. "She's the head teacher. Unfortunately, she doesn't own the school. It would be a different place if she did. No, Mr Brocklehurst is in charge of the school. He's a clergyman."

"Miss Temple is a good person, isn't she?" I asked next.

"Yes, she's very good and very clever."

I asked the girl a lot more questions, and I discovered that her name was Helen Burns. She had been at Lowood for two years, and her mother was dead.

I was happy because she had spoken kindly to me, but I was also anxious. During our talk Helen had coughed a lot.

Life at Lowood was harder than at Gateshead Hall, but I did not want to return to my aunt's house. I had some difficulties at first because the lessons were new to me. But soon I began to understand and enjoy them. I had only one problem – I was always hungry. But all the girls at Lowood had the same problem.

Soon Helen Burns and I were friends. She taught me to have courage when there were difficulties. She herself was very ill and her coughing grew worse as the winter continued. She had a terrible illness, and she would never get better. But she never talked about it. She was the kindest and nicest person I had ever met.

About three weeks after I arrived at Lowood something terrible happened. It showed me how good and kind Helen was. We were all sitting in class one day when Mr Brocklehurst came into the room with Miss Temple. I was very frightened. I had begun to feel happy at Lowood. Most of the girls and the teachers had been kind to me. Unlike Mrs Reed, they did not think that I was a wicked child.

I tried to sit still so that Mr Brocklehurst would not notice me. But then I dropped my book with a loud noise. I wanted to die! I was so ashamed.

Mr Brocklehurst turned to me, and his eyes were cold and hard. "Oh – I see it is the new girl – come here, Jane Eyre. I have something to say about you."

I was standing in front of Mr Brocklehurst when I heard Miss Temple say very quietly, "Don't be afraid, Jane. I saw that it was an accident." How kind she was to me at that terrible moment!

Mr Brocklehurst pointed to a stool and said, "Stand on that stool!" For the next ten minutes, he told all the teachers and girls everything he knew about me. "She tells lies," he said. "The school must not talk to such a wicked girl." As he left the room, he said loudly, "Jane Eyre must stand on that stool for half an hour and no one must speak to her until tomorrow morning!"

I was so ashamed. I wanted to die. "Now everyone will hate me," I thought. But suddenly I saw Helen. She was smiling at me. She wanted to give me courage.

I did not leave my stool until everyone had gone for tea. Then I sat down in a corner and wept. I felt so unhappy and lonely. Soon afterwards, Helen came into the school-room again.

"Jane," she said, "you mustn't cry, you know. We don't all have Mr Brocklehurst's opinion of you. In fact, I'm sure that many of us feel sorry for you."

Until that moment, Mr Brocklehurst had seemed a god, but now he seemed less important.

Mr Brocklehurst makes Jane stand on a stool

"Listen, Jane," she continued. "You know that you aren't a wicked person. So Mr Brocklehurst's opinion of you isn't very important. Don't think so much about other people's opinions."

And so at last I grew quiet. Miss Temple came into the room. "Please come to my room, Jane," she said. "I want to talk to you. Come with us, Helen, if you like."

Miss Temple's room was warm and comfortable. We sat down in front of the fire. "Do you feel better now, Jane? Have you wept enough?"

"Not really, Miss Temple," I answered sadly.

"Why not?" she asked.

"Because Mr Brocklehurst's words were not true. But now you will all think that I am really wicked. You'll hate me for it," I replied.

"Jane," said Miss Temple quietly, "please tell me your story of your life with your aunt. Then I'll decide whether Mr Brocklehurst's words are true or not."

And so I told her everything. I was careful not to say anything that was not true. When I came to the part about Dr Lloyd, she stopped me.

"I've heard of Dr Lloyd, Jane," she said. "And I know that he's a good and honest man. I'll write to him and ask him about you. If his story is the same as yours, I'll tell everyone that you aren't a wicked child. I give you my promise, Jane. Now, you two are my visitors tonight. You must have some tea with me."

A week later, Dr Lloyd replied to Miss Temple's letter. His story agreed with mine and Miss Temple kept her promise. She told everyone that Mr Brocklehurst's words about Jane Eyre were not true. And from that moment I began to love my life at Lowood.

Chapter 3
Leaving Lowood

As winter changed to spring, illness came to Lowood. The girls were weak after a cold, wet winter and the bad food that Mr Brocklehurst had ordered. Typhus quickly attacked one girl after another. Soon forty-five of the eighty girls at the school were in bed. Many of them died of typhus that spring. The teachers worked day and night. They did not have time to give classes now. Those of us who were well could do as we wished. We spent long days in the country. We had no fear of Mr Brocklehurst now. He never came near the school.

Helen was very ill at that time, too. She did not have typhus, but I knew that her illness was very serious. Sometimes at night I thought I could hear her coughing.

One evening at the beginning of June, I saw the doctor's carriage outside the front door.

"Someone must be very ill," I thought. "Dr Bates doesn't usually come so late."

For some strange reason, I immediately thought of Helen. "I must see her now!" I said to myself.

"Oh – is it you, Jane?" she asked. "How good it is to hear your voice!"

I kissed her and her face felt cold. She was thinner but her smile was still the same.

"I had to see you," I said. "I heard you were ill."

"You came to say goodbye, Jane," she replied. "You're just in time, I think."

"But – you aren't going anywhere, are you?" I asked.

She could not answer at that moment because she began to cough. Later she said, "Don't be sad, Jane. I'm

12

going to God. I shall be happy."

Helen died during the night. My best friend was gone.

After the typhus had gone, a number of changes were made at the school. At last, the world outside learnt about Lowood. The school was moved to a better place, less cold and wet. Our food and clothes were better, too. I remained there for eight years – six as one of the girls and two as a teacher. I enjoyed my life as a teacher. I have always been plain – not at all good-looking – and small, but the girls seemed to like me. By the end, Miss Temple was not only my teacher but also my friend.

After I had been at the school for about eight years, Miss Temple married a clergyman. She went to live far from Lowood. Lowood would never be the same again. I decided to put an advertisement in a newspaper.

A young woman wishes to find work with a family where the children are under fourteen years old. She is able to teach English, French, drawing and music. Please write to J E, The Post Office, Lowood.

One week later, I went to the Post Office. There was only one letter for me. It was short. It came from a Mrs Fairfax who lived at Thornfield Hall, near Millcote. She wanted a governess to teach a little girl of nine. She asked me to write and tell her more about myself.

I had to tell the new head teacher about my plans. I asked her to tell Mr Brocklehurst. Mr Brocklehurst said that I must tell Mrs Reed, and so I wrote her a letter.

Her answer was this: "Jane Eyre may do as she wishes. I do not want to know anything about her or her life." After that I wrote to Mrs Fairfax and said that I would be glad to come.

Chapter 4
Thornfield

The journey to Millcote was long and tiring. I arrived at the George Hotel, Millcote, at eight o'clock in the evening. An old man called John met me at the hotel. He drove me to Thornfield Hall in a carriage.

A woman servant opened the door and took me to meet Mrs Fairfax. Her room was very warm and comfortable.

Mrs Fairfax spoke to me very kindly. "Come and sit near the fire, my dear. You must be cold and tired after your journey. Will you have some supper?"

As soon as I saw her, I knew she was a kind person. She looked after Thornfield Hall, but she did not own it. I was very tired and soon Mrs Fairfax showed me to my room.

I slept well that night. I was happy because I had arrived safely at the start of my new life.

When I woke up the next morning, the sun was shining brightly and my little room looked friendly and safe. I dressed and went downstairs to explore my new home. I went out into the garden to look at the house from the outside. It stood completely alone, with hills all around it. In the distance I could just see a small village.

While I was standing outside, Mrs Fairfax appeared. "Good morning," she said, and she smiled kindly. "How do you like Thornfield?"

"Very much," I replied. "It's a beautiful place."

"But I'm afraid it won't remain beautiful if Mr Rochester continues to travel so much away from home."

"Who's Mr Rochester?" I asked.

"He owns Thornfield Hall, of course," said Mrs Fairfax, and then she laughed. "How stupid I am! I forgot to

14

tell you his name!"

"Am I going to teach his daughter?" I asked her next.

"No," Mrs Fairfax answered. "Mr Rochester brought her here from France about six months ago. She's an orphan. When her mother died, Mr Rochester promised to look after the child. Her name is Adèle Varens."

Just then the little girl came out of the house. Mrs Fairfax told me about the difficulties they had had when Adèle first arrived. At that time neither she nor her servant, Sophie, spoke any English at all. And at Thornfield Hall only Mr Rochester could speak French.

"But Adèle's learning English quite fast," Mrs Fairfax said.

I decided to speak to Adèle in French at first, and this pleased her a lot. During breakfast she told me about her life in France. She was only nine years old, but sometimes I almost forgot that she was a child.

After breakfast we went to the library for our lessons. I found that Adèle was not an especially clever child, but she was not stupid either. She had not had a governess before, and she found the lessons difficult at first.

Before lunch, Mrs Fairfax took me to see the rest of the inside of the house. She showed me many beautiful rooms, but I thought it needed life and people.

"What kind of man is Mr Rochester?" I dared to ask Mrs Fairfax as we walked through the house.

"He has always been very kind to me," she answered. "I've worked for him for a long time. But some people say that he's rather strange."

"Oh, why?" I asked.

"It's difficult to explain," Mrs Fairfax replied. "When you speak to him you can never be certain whether he's laughing or not."

Mrs Fairfax could not tell me any more about Mr Rochester. I wanted to know more, but I had to wait to meet him myself.

By this time we had reached the third floor of Thornfield. The rooms here were smaller and darker. They were a little frightening.

"Does anyone sleep up here?" I asked.

"Oh, no. The servants have some rooms high up on the other side of the house, but no one sleeps here. If Thornfield had a ghost, perhaps it would live here!" and Mrs Fairfax laughed.

At that moment we came to a small door which opened on to the roof. We went outside into the sunshine, and there was the most wonderful view of the hills.

As we went back into the house, I heard a strange and very frightening noise. It was neither a laugh nor a cry.

"Mrs Fairfax!" I cried. "What was that terrible noise? Did you hear it? Who is it?"

"Oh, it's nothing," she answered. "Perhaps it was one of the servants." She did not look frightened at all. "Grace Poole often comes up here to help the other girls with the sewing."

The noise came again. It was a kind of laugh, but there was no happiness in it. Then a door opened in front of us and a woman came out. She did not look strange or frightening at all.

"You were making too much noise, Grace," Mrs Fairfax said. "Remember what I told you." Then she turned to me and asked, "How did you find Adèle this morning? Is she a clever child?"

And so we talked about Adèle until we were downstairs again.

Chapter 5
Mr Rochester

My life at Thornfield continued as quietly as it had begun.
Mrs Fairfax was a good, kind woman and Adèle was a
good child. She began to do her lessons quite well.

One day in January, Adèle had a bad cold and we could
not have any lessons. Mrs Fairfax had written a letter and I
offered to go to the village to post it for her. The village of
Hay was only about two miles away.

The road to Hay was uphill, and after a time I stopped to
rest. While I was standing there, I heard the sound of a
horse in the distance. Then suddenly I saw a large black
and white dog in front of me. Next came a man riding a
horse. They went past very quickly and I continued my
walk. But I heard a great noise, and I saw that the horse
had fallen on the icy road. The man was lying on the
ground and the dog was running around him, making a lot
of noise. I went to try to help.

By this time the horse was standing up again, but the
man was still lying on the ground.

"Can I help you, sir?" I asked.

"No, no. Just stand on one side, away from the horse,"
he answered, almost rudely.

"But, sir, if you're hurt, I can go the village to get help,"
I continued.

"No, thank you. I'm all right," he replied. He tried to
stand up, but I could see that his leg hurt him a lot.

He was about forty years old. For some strange reason,
I did not feel afraid of this stranger. Perhaps if he had been
a good-looking man, I would have been afraid. Perhaps if
he had been very polite, I would have been more uneasy.

But he was neither good-looking nor polite, and so I repeated my offer of help.

"Sir, I can't leave you here alone so late in the day. I must help you!"

"All right," he agreed. "If you give me your hand, I'll be able to stand up."

His leg hurt him a lot, but in the end he stood up. Then he caught his horse.

"And now, young woman," he said. "It's late for you to be out alone. Where do you live?"

"Down there," I answered, and I pointed to Thornfield Hall, below us in the valley.

"Who owns that house?" he asked me next.

"Mr Rochester does," I replied.

"Do you know Mr Rochester?" was his next question.

"No, I've never seen him," I answered.

"You aren't a servant at that house, are you?" he asked me next.

"No, sir. I'm the governess. I teach the little girl there."

"Ah, yes, the governess, the governess. I had forgotten the governess," he said to himself quietly. "Well, now, you must hurry home, young lady, before it gets dark."

"I'm just going to the village to post a letter, and then I'll return home," I answered.

"Well, hurry, and return as fast as you can," and he rode off towards Thornfield, while I continued to the village.

The downstairs rooms were all brightly lit when I returned to the house. I heard voices – Adèle's, Mrs Fairfax's and a man's deep voice. What had happened? Who had arrived at Thornfield?

I went upstairs to Mrs Fairfax's room. There, in front of the fire, was a great black and white dog. It was the one I had seen on the road to Hay. Then I understood – my stranger was Mr Rochester of Thornfield Hall.

I did not see Mr Rochester again until the evening of the following day. Then Mrs Fairfax told me that Mr Rochester had asked Adèle and me to have tea with him.

When we went into the sitting room, he did not even look at us! However, I had understood from our first meeting that Mr Rochester was not a very polite man, and so I was not hurt. I sat down and waited. Mrs Fairfax started to talk about the weather, but Mr Rochester replied only that he would like some tea. Adèle asked him about the present that he had promised her, but he did not answer.

After about half an hour Mr Rochester suddenly turned to me. He began to ask me about my life. He asked me about my family, about Lowood and about Mr Brocklehurst. He had heard about Mr Brocklehurst before. I hope I gave him honest answers, even about Mr Brocklehurst.

He asked me about my drawings and paintings. I showed him some and he asked who had helped me with them. He seemed surprised when I answered, "No one."

As we went upstairs, I asked Mrs Fairfax about Mr Rochester.

"Perhaps he seems rude to you," she said. "But I've known him for so many years that I don't notice. To tell you the truth, Jane, he has had a difficult life. Perhaps that's why he's rather strange. For many years neither his father nor his brother Rowland spoke to him. They gave him no money or help. He didn't return to Thornfield until after his brother died nine years ago. Even now he doesn't spend very much time here."

Jane shows Mr Rochester her drawings and paintings

I saw little of Mr Rochester during the next few days. Once or twice I met him on the stairs or in the garden. Sometimes he smiled and said, "Good morning, Miss Eyre," but at other times he did not even notice me.

Then, one evening, he sent for Mrs Fairfax, Adèle and me. As soon as we went into the sitting room, Mr Rochester gave Adèle her present. Then he told her to go away with Mrs Fairfax and open it.

His first question to me was, "Miss Eyre, do you think that I'm good-looking?"

My answer was spoken before I could stop it, "No, sir."

"Well –" he cried, and then he laughed. "You are a strange young woman. You seem so quiet and polite. And then suddenly you give me a really honest answer. I like that. You're right to be honest. I hate people who are too anxious to please."

Adèle and I were walking in the garden one afternoon when we met Mr Rochester. He told Adèle to go and play with his dog, Pilot, and then he began to tell me about Adèle's mother. He had met her in Paris. He had loved her greatly. But she had died, and Adèle had been left alone in the world. Mr Rochester had decided to bring the child to England. He said that she was not his daughter, but she had no family and she needed a home.

We talked for a long time about Paris and Adèle's mother. While we did so, Mr Rochester often raised his eyes to the third floor of the house. I had the feeling that he wanted to escape from something at Thornfield. His eyes were full of hatred and sadness as he looked up.

After that meeting in the garden Mr Rochester began to behave differently towards me. When we met, he seemed pleased.

Chapter 6
Fire!

To Mrs Fairfax's surprise, Mr Rochester had already been at Thornfield for nearly two months. He and I had had many long talks, but I still did not know what he hated about Thornfield. Most of the time he seemed happy, especially when we were talking in the evenings. But the look of hatred and sadness that I had seen in the garden often returned.

One night I lay in bed and wondered for the hundredth time what secret Mr Rochester kept in his heart. Suddenly I heard a noise outside my bedroom door. It was something between a laugh and a cry, but it was very quiet. I had heard the sound before.

Then I heard footsteps. They went up to the third floor. I got up very quietly and went out of my room.

"Was that really Grace Poole's laugh?" I asked myself.

The air outside my room was full of smoke. I thought it came from Mr Rochester's room. His door was open and I could smell burning. I ran to Mr Rochester's room. He was asleep, but his bed was on fire.

"Wake up! Wake up!" I cried. But he did not move. I had to do something quickly. I rushed to get some water. I threw it over Mr Rochester's bed. The fire went out. At that moment Mr Rochester woke up.

"What's the matter? What has happened? Why am I wet?" he shouted angrily.

"Sir, your bed was on fire. I threw water over you to stop it," I answered.

"Is that you, Jane Eyre?" he asked. "What are you doing here in the middle of the night?"

"Oh, please get up, sir," I cried. "Something terrible has happened."

"What is it? Who did it?" he asked.

I told him what I had seen and heard. He listened carefully. Then he said, "Jane, I'm going to leave you here for a few minutes. Stay here until I return."

I heard his footsteps go upstairs to the third floor. He was away for a long time and I began to feel frightened.

When he returned at last, his face was white.

He said, "That strange laugh that you heard tonight – have you ever heard it before?"

"Yes, sir," I replied. "There's a woman called Grace Poole who helps with the needlework here. She works on the third floor. I've sometimes heard her laugh there."

"Yes, Jane. You're right. You heard Grace Poole again tonight. There are times when she goes mad, poor woman. But she's better now, and she won't come downstairs again. I don't want you to tell anyone about tonight. I don't want to frighten the servants."

"No, sir. I promise I won't say a word to anyone," I answered.

"Jane!" he said, and he took my hand. "I knew when I first saw you that you would help me one day. Your eyes and your smile told me. I've heard about people who meet and know immediately that their lives are joined in some way. Now I know that these things are true. My dear Jane, good night."

I left him and returned to my room. I could not sleep because I felt so happy. Mr Rochester had needed me, and I had been able to help him. For the first time he had called me Jane, not Miss Eyre. I began to hope that one day he would love me, as I already loved him. It was only a faint hope because I knew I was small and not at all beautiful.

Chapter 7
Miss Ingram

The next morning the servants were cleaning up after the fire. Mr Rochester had not told Mrs Fairfax the truth about it. He said a candle had caused the fire.

I was surprised to see Grace Poole in Mr Rochester's room that morning. I decided to ask her some questions. I wanted to know if she had really caused the fire. Her answers did not seem mad. It was very strange. Last night she had tried to kill Mr Rochester, but now she was working quietly in his room.

I wanted to see Mr Rochester very much, but at the same time I was rather frightened. Had I dreamt that he had held my hand? Had he really called me his dear Jane?

During the midday meal, Mrs Fairfax said, "Mr Rochester has had a fine day for his journey, I think." .

"Journey!" I cried. "Has Mr Rochester gone somewhere? I didn't know that he planned to leave Thornfield."

"Yes, he left this morning immediately after breakfast. He has gone to visit the Eshtons, some friends who live on the other side of Millcote. People say that there are a lot of grand ladies and gentlemen there at the moment."

"Is he coming back tonight?" I asked quietly.

"Oh, no," Mrs Fairfax replied. "I think he plans to stay for at least a week. Mr Rochester is a great favourite with the ladies at these parties." And Mrs Fairfax began to tell me about all the clever and beautiful ladies at the Eshtons' house. She talked about one more than all the others – Miss Blanche Ingram. "People think that she and Mr Rochester may marry one day," she said at last.

Later that night, when I was alone in my room, I tried to

think clearly about Mr Rochester and myself. I decided that I had been a stupid young woman. After last night, I had dared to hope that Mr Rochester would love me. I saw now that I had been a fool. I was a plain little governess whom Mr Rochester paid. How could he love me?

A week passed. Then, one morning, a letter arrived for Mrs Fairfax.

"Well," she said when she had read it, "we'll be very busy for the next few weeks at least!"

I tried not to show my feelings, and I asked quietly, "Mr Rochester isn't coming home, is he?"

"Yes, he is," she replied. "On Thursday, he says. He's bringing a lot of grand people with him, too. We're going to be busy, Jane."

Adèle was very excited about all the grand ladies and gentlemen who were coming. She saw them first as they rode up to the house. There were four people on horses in front, and behind them there were two coaches. Mr Rochester was riding one of the horses in front and beside him I saw a beautiful woman.

"That's Miss Ingram," Mrs Fairfax told me. "She's more beautiful than ever!"

Mr Rochester sent a message upstairs. He wanted Adèle and me to go to the sitting room after dinner. I did not want to go, but Mrs Fairfax told me that Mr Rochester had asked for me especially. I was a little frightened when we went down – how would all these grand people behave towards me, a poor governess? But Adèle was very excited. At last she was going to see all the beautiful ladies!

The visitors had not finished dinner when we went into the sitting room. I sat down in a corner. If possible, I did not want the visitors to notice me.

Chapter 8
The fortune teller

Mr Rochester did not have time to speak to me in the days which followed. I went to the sitting room every evening, but no one noticed me in my corner. The days passed, and the weeks, too. Thornfield was a happy, busy place then, but not for me.

One day Mr Rochester had work to do. He was out all day, and by the evening he had not returned. Suddenly we heard a carriage outside. But it was not Mr Rochester who came to the door. It was a complete stranger.

"I'm sorry that my friend Mr Rochester is out," he said as he came in. "Please allow me to wait here for him. I have had a very long, hard journey."

He was about Mr Rochester's age, tall and quite good-looking. He seemed polite, but there was something weak in his face, which I did not like. During the talk which followed I learned that he lived in the West Indies. He had met Mr Rochester there many years before.

At that moment one of the servants came in. She said that there was a fortune teller outside.

When they heard this, all the ladies were very excited. "Ooh, yes! We must have our fortunes told! It'll be such fun to know about the future!"

"She only wants to see the young ladies who aren't married," the servant said next. "She won't come in here. Each lady must go to the library alone."

Blanche Ingram went first. She returned more than a quarter of an hour later. Everyone wanted to know what the fortune teller had said. But Miss Ingram did not tell them anything. I was surprised because she usually talked

so much. What had the fortune teller told her? Had she
learnt something which she had not wanted to hear?

The other three young women were allowed to see the
old woman together. Their visit was much shorter than
Miss Ingram's. Unlike her, they were laughing and talking
excitedly when they returned.

"She knew everything about us!" one of them cried.
"Our families, our lives, who we love most – everything!"

While they were telling everyone about the fortune
teller, the servant returned. She came to speak to me.
"Please, Miss Eyre, the fortune teller says that there's
another young woman in the room. I think she means you.
She wants to see you, too."

The library was quiet and dark when I went in. The fire
gave the only light in the room, but I did not feel afraid.
The old woman was sitting near the fire. She was wearing
a big red coat and a large hat. I could not see her face
because it was in shadow.

"You want me to tell your fortune, do you?" she asked.

"Yes, if you want to tell me it," I replied.

She laughed quietly. "Well," she began. "You're cold,
you're sick, and you're stupid."

"What do you mean?" I asked her.

"You're alone, and so you're cold. You're trying to stop
the highest and best feelings that a woman can have. And
so you're sick. You won't allow these feelings to come near
you. And so you're stupid."

"But you could say that about many women," I said.
"Especially about women who live and work in big houses
away from their own families."

"No," she replied. "There are very few women like you.
You are very near happiness. But you won't reach out and

27

touch it because you are afraid."

"I don't understand," I said. "Please explain what you mean. Here, look at my hand. That's how your people usually tell fortunes."

"I'd rather look at your face," she said. "Come nearer. I want to see your face in the firelight."

I went and sat near her.

"I wonder what you feel in the sitting room with those grand people every evening. Are you unhappy? Or do you hope that your life will change one day?"

"I'm not unhappy," I answered. "And my only hope is that I'll be able to start a school of my own one day."

"Everyone in this house is watching two people at the moment, aren't they?" she asked next.

"Yes, you're right," I answered.

"What have you seen in the two faces?" she asked. "Is it love?" She was looking straight into my eyes.

"No," I answered. "I haven't seen love there."

"But those two are going to marry, aren't they?"

"Yes, everyone says that Mr Rochester will marry Miss Ingram soon," I replied. "But I didn't come here to listen to their fortunes," I added.

"Your fortune isn't clear to me at the moment," the old woman said. "Come closer. I want to look at your face again." I moved nearer and she began to talk very quietly. "Her eyes are shining; they're full of feeling. Her mouth is serious now; but it can laugh and smile with happiness. Her face tells me that she is strong and brave. She'll decide what is right, and then she'll do it. She'll hide her love if she must . . ." The old woman continued like this for some minutes. At the end she cried, "Oh, Jane, stand up! Leave me! I mustn't say more! My game is finished!"

Was I dreaming? Was I asleep or awake? The old

woman's voice had changed now. I knew that voice as well as my own. She took off her hat and coat, and there stood Mr Rochester!

"I don't understand, sir. What did you want to discover about me? I've told you a lot of things that you ought not to know ..." Here I stopped. Had Mr Rochester learnt my secret? Did he know that I loved him?

"But, Jane, you told me nothing bad – nothing that I didn't know already. Don't be angry with me, please. What are they doing in the sitting room?"

"Talking about you, I think." And I laughed. Then I remembered. "A stranger has arrived."

"A stranger! Who is it?" he said.

"His name is Mason and he comes from the West Indies, I think," I replied.

The smile left Mr Rochester's face. He took my hand and held it tightly. "Mason!" he breathed. "The West Indies! Oh no! Oh no!"

"Are you ill, sir?" I asked, because his face was very white.

"Jane, Jane, this is terrible!" he continued. "I wish that you and I were alone together on an island, far away from all these troubles and dangers. Oh, what shall I do? What shall I do?"

"Can I help you, sir? I'd give my life to serve you," I told him quietly.

"My little friend," he said. "If I need your help, I'll come to you, I promise."

"But can't I help you now?" I asked.

"Yes," he said. "Go and find Mason and tell him that I'm back. Then bring him here, please."

I found Mason in the dining room. After I had taken him to the library, I went to bed.

Chapter 9
Danger in the night

I did not sleep for long. Suddenly there was a terrible cry. The sound came from the third floor. Then I heard another cry from above my head. It was much quieter this time. "Help! Help! Rochester, help me!" Immediately, a door opened and I heard footsteps.

I got dressed quickly and went out of my room. All the visitors were up.

Then Mr Rochester appeared. "Don't be afraid, my friends. There's no danger. One of the servants has had a bad dream. She thought she saw a ghost. That's all. Now, please go back to bed and try to sleep."

Slowly everyone returned to their rooms. I did not sleep. I waited to see if Mr Rochester needed me. I heard nothing for about half an hour. Then there was a very quiet knock at my door.

"Are you awake, Jane?" Mr Rochester asked.

"Yes, sir," I answered. "Do you need me?"

"Yes, come quickly and don't make a sound," was his answer. "Bring some water and a cloth if you can."

I followed Mr Rochester up to the third floor. "Jane, you're going to see something terrible. You won't be afraid if you see blood, will you?" He opened a door.

I saw Mr Mason on a bed. His eyes were closed and his face was white. One of his arms was covered in blood.

"Hold the candle, Jane," Mr Rochester said. Then he began to wash Mr Mason's arm and face. The poor man opened his eyes and said very weakly, "Am I going to die?"

"No, no, Mason. It isn't serious," Mr Rochester answered. "I'm going to get the doctor now." Then he turned to me and said, "Jane, I'm going to leave you with this gentleman for a time. You mustn't speak to him while I'm away. And Mason, you mustn't speak to Miss Eyre, either," he added.

I tried not to be frightened after he had gone, but it was difficult. From the next room I could hear Grace Poole's strange noises.

Daylight came at last. Mr Rochester came in with the doctor from the village.

"Now, Dr Carter," he said. "We must hurry. The man isn't too ill to move, is he?"

"No, sir. His arm isn't seriously hurt," the doctor replied. And to Mr Mason, "You'll soon be all right."

"She has killed me," the poor man answered.

"No, no," Dr Carter said. "You've lost a lot of blood, that's all."

"But she bit me like a wild animal."

"I told you not to talk to her," Mr Rochester said. "She's a dangerous woman."

"But I thought I could help," Mr Mason answered.

"You thought! You thought! You fool!" Mr Rochester cried.

By a quarter to six, Mr Mason and Dr Carter had left Thornfield. Mr Mason's last words were, "Take care of her, Rochester. Be kind to her." What did he mean?

When they had gone, Mr Rochester took my hand gently. "Oh, Jane – I wish this were the end of it all," he said. "Come with me into the garden. I can't go back to the house yet."

And so we went and sat under one of the trees. The sun was rising and the garden looked wonderful in the early morning light.

"This has been a strange night for you, Jane

Rochester began. "I'm sorry that you had to be part of it. Were you very frightened when I left you with Mason?"

"Yes, sir. I could hear strange noises. I was afraid that someone would come in from the next room. Grace Poole was in there, wasn't she?"

"I can't tell you at the moment, Jane. But I'll tell you a story. A long time ago, a young man went to another land. While he was there, he made a big mistake. The results of this mistake followed him for the rest of his life. He travelled all over the world and did many stupid things to try to forget it. But he could not. At last he returned home. He thought that his life was finished, but he met a new friend there – someone who changed him. With this new person, he began to think that life was good again. The first mistake remained and can never be forgotten. He ought not to stay with this new friend, but he wants to. He wants to live again and to try to forget the past. Is he right, Jane?"

I could not say yes. I knew that Mr Rochester was telling me about himself. I also knew that I was the "new friend". I did not know what his past mistake had been, but I felt it was very serious. If he stayed with me, his new friend, he would do wrong. My heart was sad, and he knew it.

Mr

Chapter 10
Mrs Reed dies

The next afternoon I received a letter from Gateshead. It was from my cousin Eliza. I had heard nothing from the Reeds since I had left Gateshead nearly nine years before. Eliza had written because her mother was dying and had asked to see me. I did not want to go, but I knew that I must, because Mrs Reed was dying.

I went to Gateshead the next day. Bessie was very pleased to see me again, but my cousins, Georgiana and Eliza, were not friendly. They told me that their brother John had died in London a few months before. Some people said that he had killed himself. Their mother had started to be ill when she heard about her favourite child.

I saw Mrs Reed later that evening, but she did not know me. I went to her room each day and sat there for many hours. At last she said, "Is that you, Jane Eyre?"

"Yes, it is," I replied.

"Go to my desk," she said, "and get the old letter which you'll find there. Read it."

I found the letter. It said:

Dear Mrs Reed,

Please will you send me the address of my niece, Jane Eyre. I now live in Madeira and would like my niece to come here. I am an old man now, and I have no children of my own. I want Jane Eyre to come and live with me as my daughter. When I die, everything I own will be hers.

Yours sincerely,
John Eyre

The date on the letter was three years earlier.

"Why did you never tell me about this letter?" I asked Mrs Reed angrily.

"Because I hated you. I didn't want you to find your uncle. I didn't want you to live a comfortable life while my children were poor." She stopped and began to cough terribly. "Water – give me water," she breathed.

"Mrs Reed," I said as I gave her the water, "forget all this hatred."

But she was not listening to me. She began to speak again. "I wrote to your uncle and told him that you had died of typhus at Lowood. I didn't want you to be happy. You were such a wicked child. I hated you then, and I hate you still."

I waited, but she did not say anything else. I left the room after some minutes.

Mrs Reed died that night.

Chapter 11
I agree to marry Mr Rochester

Mr Rochester was alone at Thornfield when I returned there. I went to the sitting room every evening, and while Adèle played with Pilot, Mr Rochester and I had many long talks. I had never loved him so much before.

One evening in the middle of June, I went out into the garden alone. Adèle was tired and had gone to bed early. After the hot day, the garden was cool and quiet. I was walking along one of the paths, when I saw Mr Rochester in front of me. I turned to go back into the house. But he had seen me. As I walked away, he suddenly said to me, "Come and look at this rose, Jane. Isn't it wonderful? I've never seen such a beautiful rose in England before."

It was indeed a beautiful rose. I said so and then I turned to go away. But Mr Rochester stopped me and said, "Please, Jane, stay outside with me. It's such a wonderful evening."

I knew that I ought not to stay outside with Mr Rochester. But I could not think of a reason to give for leaving him. As we walked slowly down the path, Mr Rochester began to talk about his home. "Thornfield is a beautiful place in the summer, isn't it, Jane? Will you be sorry to leave it?"

"Yes – yes, sir."

"Why, Jane?"

"Because I love Thornfield, sir. Because I've been happy here. Because, for the first time in my life, I haven't been afraid. But most important of all, because I've known you, sir. And now that I must leave ..."

"Why must you leave?" he asked suddenly.

"Because you have just said so. Because you're going to marry Miss Ingram," I answered.

"Jane," he cried. "You know that I've never loved Miss Ingram. You know that she has never loved me. She hasn't spoken to me for the last month. She has heard that I'm not very rich after all. Jane – you're the one I love – please be my wife. Say that you'll be mine."

"If you really love me, I will indeed be your wife – Edward," I added. I used his first name for the first time.

"Jane, my love," Mr Rochester said, "I've loved you from the first moment I saw you. But I didn't know if you loved me. Now I think you really do love me." He took me in his arms. "God forgive me!" he cried. "I have her and will keep her with me for ever! No man shall stop me!"

"There is no one to stop you, Edward," I said. "I have no family."

"Yes, yes," he answered, but I do not think he really heard me. If I had loved him less, his words would have made me anxious. But I did not think then.

I asked Mr Rochester to tell Mrs Fairfax immediately of our plans to marry, and he did. She was so surprised that she could not speak. Later when I spoke to her alone, she seemed anxious. She told me to be careful.

Adèle was very happy and excited when she heard about our plans. And I was happy that she was happy.

Mr Rochester wanted us to marry in a month's time. I agreed. The month passed very quickly and I was very, very happy.

I had only one problem during that month. Mr Rochester wanted to give me beautiful new dresses and jewellery, but I refused them. It was unfortunate that I owned nothing. I had only what Mr Rochester gave me. I did not like this at all. Then I remembered my Uncle John in Madeira. He had told Mrs Reed that everything he owned would be mine when he died. And so I wrote to him. I told him that I was going to marry Mr Rochester. If I had some money of my own, I would feel happier.

And so the month before the wedding passed. My life at Thornfield did not change. I continued to eat my meals with Mrs Fairfax, and to see Mr Rochester only in the evenings. The only thing that changed was my love for Mr Rochester. It grew and grew until he was my whole world.

Just before the wedding, Mr Rochester had to go to one of his farms about twenty miles away. He had some important business there which could not wait. By the evening I had done everything. Even my travelling cases were ready, because we planned to leave for Europe immediately after the wedding. I sat down to wait for Mr Rochester, but I could not sit still. I was too excited. I felt very hot and so I decided to go outside into the garden. Something had happened which worried me – or at least, it made me anxious. I wanted to tell Mr Rochester about it.

I began to walk along the road to meet my love. At last I heard a horse in the distance. Then I saw Mr Rochester on his horse. Pilot was running beside him. Thank God! My sad thoughts left me. I ran forward to meet him.

"Well!" he cried when he saw me. "Can't you live one day without me?" and he laughed. "Perhaps you really do love me, my precious one!"

I climbed up on the horse and sat in front of him. As we rode back to Thornfield together, Mr Rochester said, "Is anything wrong, Jane? Has something happened while I've been away?"

"Nothing very important, Edward," I answered. "I

went to bed early last night, but I woke up in the middle of the night and saw a light in front of me. I thought at first that it was daylight and then I realised I was wrong. It was a candle. I could hear noises in the room and I saw the figure of a woman. I called out to her. But there was no answer. The figure moved towards the window. Then I saw that it wasn't Mrs Fairfax, nor any of the servants – not even Grace Poole."

"Who was it then?" Mr Rochester asked.

"I don't know," I answered. "She was a tall, large woman with long black hair. She was wearing a white dress."

"Could you see her face?" he asked.

"Not immediately, Edward," I replied. "She went over to the place where my dress and veil for the wedding were hanging. Then I saw her face. It was terrible – very dark with great red eyes. Oh, Edward, she took my veil and tore it in two pieces. Then she took the candle and left the room. When I woke next it was day."

"My dear Jane, this was another dream, I think," Mr Rochester said quietly.

"No, sir. It wasn't a dream. It was real. I found my veil on the floor this morning when I got up. It was in two pieces."

"Oh, my poor dear," Mr Rochester cried when he heard this. "What terrible thing came near you last night? Thank God you weren't hurt."

"But, Edward, who was it?" I asked. "Can you explain it?"

"Jane, I can't now. But after tomorrow I'll never leave you, and tonight I promise I'll hear you if you call me."

Chapter 12
At the church

Next morning, we left the house. No one else came with us because Mr Rochester did not want them. The church was very near and we walked there – in fact we almost ran. Mr Rochester was in a great hurry. As we went into the church I noticed two strangers outside. I did not see them clearly, and I am sure that Mr Rochester did not notice them at all.

The wedding began. Then, almost immediately, I saw one of the strangers. He had come into the church and was walking towards us.

"Stop, sir!" he said to the clergyman. "The wedding cannot continue. Mr Rochester already has a wife."

My heart stood still when I heard his words. I looked at Mr Rochester. His eyes were as hard as rock. He did not speak immediately. He took my hand and held it tightly.

"Who are you?" he asked the stranger.

"My name is Briggs," the man answered.

"And you say that I have a wife?" Mr Rochester continued. "Explain your words, sir."

"I have here a paper which says that on 20th October, 18—, you, Edward Rochester, married Bertha Mason in Jamaica. This paper was given to me by that woman's brother, Richard Mason. I am his lawyer in London."

Mr Mason came forward very slowly. He was the man I had last seen three months before. I had seen him in that terrible room at Thornfield. His face was white and he could not speak.

"Well?" said Mr Rochester, his face red with anger. "What have you to say?"

Mr Mason drew back. Then he said, "Your wife is now at Thornfield Hall. I saw her there three months ago."

"At Thornfield Hall!" the clergyman cried. "That isn't possible. I've lived in this village for many years and I've never heard of a Mrs Rochester!"

"No, by God!" said Mr Rochester loudly. "Of course you haven't. I didn't tell the world that I had a mad wife. But I'm sure you've heard stories about a mad woman at Thornfield. Well, I tell you that that mad woman is my wife. Come – come, all of you, to Thornfield to meet her. Come and see why I wanted to escape from her."

We followed him back to Thornfield. The servants were all waiting to greet us. At the door, Mr Rochester shouted at them, "Away! All of you – go away! There has been no wedding today! It's too late! Fifteen years too late!"

We followed him as he ran upstairs to the third floor. There, he opened a door which led into the room where I had last seen Mr Mason. Then he opened another door. The room inside had no windows and was quite dark. I could see Grace Poole in a corner near the fire. She was cooking.

"Good morning, Mrs Poole," Mr Rochester cried. "How are you? And how's my wife this morning?"

"She's not so bad, sir," Grace Poole answered. "She's rather angry, but not dangerous."

And then, in the darkness, I saw her – that terrible woman who had come to my room two nights before. She looked like a wild animal. She was standing on her arms as well as her legs, and she was making strange and frightening noises like an angry dog. When she saw Mr Rochester, she ran forward.

"Oh, be careful, sir!" Grace Poole shouted. "She has seen you. Perhaps you ought to leave!"

Mr Briggs stops the wedding

"No, Mrs Poole," Mr Rochester replied. "I want these people to meet my wife."

At that moment the terrible woman ran to Mr Rochester and put her hands around his neck. It was not a sign of love. I think she wanted to kill him, and she certainly looked very strong. Mr Rochester fought with her for some minutes. Then at last he pushed her into a chair. He tied her arms and legs. Strangely, during their fight, Mr Rochester had been quite gentle with her. He wanted to hurt her as little as possible. Mr Mason had tried to leave during the fight, but Mr Rochester had ordered him to stay. And he did.

"This is my wife," Mr Rochester said when the woman was quiet again. "And this is how she has behaved towards me for fifteen years. As you can see, she's mad, and so was her mother. But no one told me that before we were married," he added, and he turned to look at Mr Mason angrily. "I've tried hard, but I can do nothing to change her." He turned to me and said, "This is the woman I love. This dear, sweet girl, who stands so quietly at the gates of hell. Now perhaps you can understand why I wanted to marry Jane Eyre. I know that I was wrong, but look at Jane – she loves me truly. She knew nothing about my first wife. She honestly thought that I was free to marry her." He stopped for a moment and then continued, "Now – go, all of you! Briggs and Mason – get out of my house for ever. You've seen the hell in which I live – now go! I never want to see you again."

Mason, the lawyer Briggs, the clergyman and I left that terrible room. Mr Rochester stayed to talk to Grace Poole. Mr Briggs spoke to me downstairs. After the things which I had just seen, his words meant nothing to me.

"Miss Eyre," he began, "you have done nothing wrong. Your uncle will be glad to hear that, I'm sure – if he's still alive when Mr Mason returns to Madeira."

"My uncle? Do you know him?" I asked.

"No, but Mr Mason does," he answered. "In fact Mr Mason was staying with him when your letter arrived there. Your uncle knew that Mr Mason had a friend called Rochester. And so when you told your uncle about your plans to marry Mr Rochester, he told Mr Mason. As you will understand, Mr Mason was very surprised. And so he told your uncle all about Mr Rochester and his sister. Your uncle was very unhappy about your future, so he sent Mr Mason back to England immediately. He asked him to try to stop the wedding. Mr Mason came to me for help because I am a lawyer in London. I was glad to give it to him. I'm also glad that we were able to stop the wedding. Your uncle is now very ill. He may not live much longer. In fact, I fear that he may already be dead. If your uncle were well, I would advise you to return to Madeira with Mr Mason. But he is not, and so I advise you to remain in England until you hear more." He turned to Mr Mason, who was sitting in a chair with his head in his hands. "Must we stay any longer, Mason?" he asked.

"No, no," Mason replied. "Quickly, let us leave immediately. I hate this terrible place."

And so they and the clergyman left Thornfield Hall before Mr Rochester came downstairs again. When they had left I began to understand the terrible thing which had happened. My heart was breaking with sadness. I went up to my room, locked the door and sat down at a table. For the first time that morning I tried to think. I did not cry – that would come later. At that moment I was too unhappy to weep.

Chapter 13
I learn the truth

Late in the afternoon, I stood up weakly. I felt ill because I had eaten nothing since breakfast. The house was very quiet. I thought sadly that everyone had forgotten me. I went to my door and opened it. As I stepped out, I fell against something. Two strong arms held me tightly. I looked up and saw Mr Rochester.

"Thank God!" he said. "You've come out at last! I've been waiting here for a long time. I've heard no sound at all. I feared that you were dead. Why didn't you come to me? Why are you so quiet? I'd rather you shouted at me, Jane. I lied to you. Why aren't you angry with me? I promise you, I didn't want to hurt you. I love you more than anything in the world. You know that, don't you? But will you ever be able to forgive me?"

I forgave him everything when I heard those words. I knew that he still loved me truly, but I could not say it.

"I'm tired and ill, Mr Rochester. I need some water," was all I could say. He said nothing. He carried me downstairs to the library. There, he gave me some wine and slowly I began to feel better.

"If I could die now. I'd be happy," I thought to myself. "I can't leave Mr Rochester – I don't want to – I can't go."

"How are you now, Jane?" Mr Rochester asked me after some minutes.

"Better, sir," I answered. "I'll soon be well."

He came and sat beside me.

"Jane," he said, "I want you to hear my story. Then I'm sure you'll understand. Will you listen?"

"I'll listen for hours if you wish," I replied.

"It'll only be for a few minutes," he said. "Jane, did you know that I had a brother, who was older than me?"

"Yes. Mrs Fairfax told me so," I said.

"Did Mrs Fairfax also tell you that my father loved his money more than anything in the world?"

"I've heard something like that," I said.

"Well, Jane. My father didn't want to divide everything he owned when he died. He wanted everything to remain the same when he was dead. And so he gave everything to my brother Rowland. But my father also hated the idea that one of his sons would be a poor man. And so he wanted me to marry a rich woman. He had an old friend, Mr Mason, who lived in the West Indies. He knew that Mr Mason had a son and a daughter. Then he heard that Mr Mason had promised to give his daughter thirty thousand pounds if she married. My father had found the answer to his problem. When I was twenty-two I was sent to the West Indies. I went to meet the woman my father had chosen for me. My father didn't tell me all this, however. He told me only that Mr Mason had a very beautiful daughter – and he was right. He told me nothing about her money or his plans for us to marry.

"Bertha Mason was indeed a fine woman. She was tall and dark, rather like Blanche Ingram. I met her many times, but always in company. I never saw her alone. She seemed to be especially fond of me, and I thought that she was being honest. All the men around her were in love with her. And I followed their example. I was young. I knew nothing about the world. I thought I loved her. Her family wanted us to marry, and, almost before I knew it, we were husband and wife. When I think of it now, I'm very ashamed. I didn't really love her, and she didn't love me, either. But I was young then and stupid."

He stopped for a moment and put his head in his hands. Then he continued. "I had never met my wife's mother. In fact I understood that she was dead. But soon I discovered that she was mad. There was also a younger brother and he was mad, too. The other brother, Richard, you know. I hate all his family, but I can't really hate him. He has always tried to be kind to his sister. My father and brother knew all about the Mason family, but they didn't tell me. They only wanted the money – they didn't care about me at all.

"When I learned that they had hidden the truth from me, I was wildly angry. My family had planned everything. They had wanted me to marry her and I had done so. I had not really chosen her. My family did not care about my happiness – and I can never forgive that. Many terrible things happened during the four years I lived with my wife. I can't and won't tell you about them now. Everything she said and did was wicked and terrible, and she grew worse each day."

Here he stopped and looked at me carefully. "Jane, you look ill. Shall I stop this terrible story now? I can finish it another day."

"No, no. Finish it now. Oh, Mr Rochester, I'm so sorry for you – so sorry," I said. "But what did you do next?"

"I wanted to die, Jane. And one hot night I decided to kill myself. My wife had been shouting at me all day. She was behaving like a wild animal. My life was hell. The air around me was hot and heavy, and I could see no end to it all. I took my gun, but at that moment a fresh wind came. Soon after there was a great storm, which left the air cool and clear. I went out into the garden. I felt that my thoughts were cooler and clearer, too. I decided to return to England. I planned to leave my wife at Thornfield with someone to look after her. Then I would travel in other lands. No one in England knew that I was married. My father had kept it secret. He was too ashamed to tell people that my wife was mad.

"And so I came back to Thornfield. I hoped that I would be able to forget at least part of my sadness. I locked my wife in the room on the third floor. She has lived there for the last ten years. I found Grace Poole to look after her. Only Grace Poole and Dr Carter knew the secret about my wife. Even Mrs Fairfax didn't know it. I'm sure that some of the servants know that there's a mystery. But none of them know the truth.

"For ten long years I visited all the big cities of Europe, but I never found a woman I could love – except Adèle's mother. And she died.

"And so, Jane, I returned to Thornfield last January. I knew life here was going to be difficult, but I wanted to be alone. And then, as I was riding from Hay, I saw a little figure by the side of the road. I didn't know then that this woman would soon be my whole world. But that, my dearest Jane, is what you are now. The rest of the story you know, Jane. You know how we came to know and love each other, and——"

"Stop, sir, please, please, don't talk about those days. My heart will break," I cried.

He put his arms out to me, but I ran away.

"Goodbye, goodbye, my love, for ever!" my heart cried as I left him.

Chapter 14
Leaving Thornfield

I got up very early the next morning. I had decided to leave Thornfield and Mr Rochester immediately. I wanted to go before any of the servants got up. When I walked past Mr Rochester's room, I could hear him. He was walking up and down. I wanted to go in and see him so much, but I knew that I must not.

"Mr Rochester," I said to myself very quietly as I passed his door. "I will love you until the day I die." Then I quickly ran from the house.

I hurried to the road which led away from Millcote. I stopped to rest for a moment when I reached the road. Soon I heard the sound of a coach in the distance. I shouted to the driver as the coach passed me. I asked him to take me with him. I offered him a pound. That was all the money I had in the world.

I travelled by coach for two days. Then I had to leave it in the middle of open country. The driver could not take me any further because I had no more money. I spent my second night away from Thornfield under the stars. Where else could I go? I had no money.

In the morning I woke up with the sun. I decided to walk along the road which led to the east. In my heart I wanted only to die. But life was with me still and I had to look for work and food.

I walked for many hours. In the early afternoon I arrived at a village. It lay in a valley and it looked quiet and friendly in the sunshine. But it was not friendly to me. I asked a lot of people where I could work, but no one would help me. I asked for food, but no one gave me any.

Late in the afternoon I walked away from the village. No one there cared about me.

I planned to sleep under the stars again. But the night was colder, and it began to rain. I walked and walked until it was very late. I felt very, very tired. Then suddenly I saw a light in the distance.

"It must be a dream," I told myself.

I started to walk towards the light and it did not go away. It came from a small house which stood alone. I was so tired that I dared to go into the garden. I could see two young women and an old woman through a little window. The two young women were reading and talking. The older one was their servant, I thought. By this time, I was very, very weak. I stood watching them for a long time. I was unable to move. At last I went to the door and knocked quietly. I heard a dog inside, and after a few minutes the old woman came to the door.

"What do you want?" she asked angrily. "Why are you out alone so late at night? It's not right."

"Please ... please," I begged. "I'm a stranger and I have no place to go. Can you give me a little bread to eat? May I sleep here?"

"I'll give you some bread, but you can't sleep here, young woman," she replied. "How do we know who you are? You may have some wicked friends near. They might come and kill us during the night."

She went inside. After some minutes, she came out again with a small piece of bread. She gave it to me and then she shut the door in my face. "Now go away!" were her last words.

"I must die then," I said quietly.

I was too weak to move from the door and

I lay down on the steps. But at that moment I heard footsteps and a man's voice.

"No, no, you won't die at my door," it said.

I could not see the man in the darkness, but the voice sounded quite young. He knocked at the door and shouted, "Hurry, Hannah, Open the door! There's a poor woman here. We must help her."

"I know, sir," replied the same old woman who had spoken to me. "I've already told her to go away. I was afraid she was dangerous," she added.

"I don't think so, Hannah," the man answered. "Help her inside. We can't leave her on the doorstep."

They both helped me to stand, and we went into the house. The two young women ran forward to meet us.

"Who is she, St John?" I heard one of them ask.

"I don't know, Diana," the man replied.

"Oh dear!" said the other young woman. "She's so white and thin. Is she just hungry or is she ill as well?"

"Just hungry, I think, Mary," the man answered.

I sat down by the fire and they gave me warm bread and milk. The man asked me some questions when I began to feel better. First he wanted to know my name. "Jane Elliott," I answered. Then he asked where I lived, if I had any friends or family, and why I was so poor. I did not want to answer these questions. I begged him to let me explain later.

Then the two young women and the man left the room. One of the young women returned about ten minutes later and spoke quietly to Hannah. "The poor girl must stay here for tonight. We can't send her out into the cold again. Help her upstairs, poor thing."

And so I found help at last. For the first time in three days I slept in a dry, comfortable bed.

Chapter 15
My new friends

I lay in that little bed for three days and nights. I was unable to move. I could hear and understand the people around me, but I could not speak.

On the third day I felt better and on the fourth day I got up in the afternoon. I went to the kitchen. Hannah was making bread there. She seemed surprised to see me. At first she was rather unfriendly, but we talked for some time and she began to change her opinion of me, I think. From her, I learned that the kind people who had saved me were called Rivers. Their father had died three weeks before. The three young people were at home for that reason. St John was a clergyman in Morton, the village where I had asked for work. Diana and Mary were both governesses with grand families in the south of England.

After about an hour the two girls came in, and we had tea in the sitting room with St John. He asked me a lot of questions, many of which I did not answer. But by the end he understood that I was an honest woman. He promised to help me find work.

My love for Diana and Mary grew from that day. They were very kind to me and we were soon good friends. I enjoyed the time I spent with them and the days flew past. We all three liked the same things – reading, painting and drawing, walking in the country. The sadness in my heart was still there, but they helped me greatly.

Almost a month had passed since I had arrived at the Rivers' house. Diana and Mary had to return to their work as governesses and St John was going back to his own

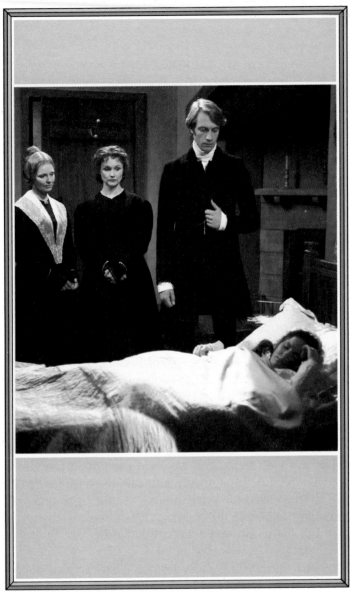

Jane is ill in bed for three days

house in Morton. I began to worry about my future.

One morning, St John said, "I have found something for you, but you may not like the idea very much. I began a school for the boys of the village about a year ago, and now I want to do the same for the girls. I've found a building for the school, and a house for the teacher. It won't be a grand school. The girls will all be from the village, and you will teach only reading, writing and needlework. But it will be useful work. Do you think that you can do it? More important – do you want to do it?"

"Yes, Mr Rivers," I replied, "I shall be very glad to do it." And I meant what I said. My life would be quiet and useful. Perhaps if I worked very hard, I would be able to forget the past.

St John seemed surprised because I had agreed so quickly. At the same time, he was pleased that I had agreed, and he smiled warmly.

On the last day of the holiday, a letter arrived for St John. He opened it and read it. Then, without a word, he gave it to Diana and Mary to read.

"Uncle John is dead!" Diana cried when she had finished the letter.

"Yes," said St John. "And he has left all his money to someone else!"

The three of them looked a little sad.

"Well, we can live without his help," Mary said quietly. "We have lived without it up to now."

St John left the room then, and Diana turned to me.

"Please don't think that we're unkind, Jane," she said. "We've never known Uncle John. He was my mother's brother, and he and my father quarrelled many, many years ago. My father lost all his money because of Uncle

John. Later in his life Uncle John became a rich man. My father hoped that he would help us when he died. He had no children of his own. But he has left all his money to someone else. Of course, he was free to give his money as he wished, but we had hoped . . ." She stopped and said no more.

And so at last, I had a home of my own. It was a very small house, but at least it was mine.

I had twenty girls on my first day at the school. None of them could write, and only three of them could read. I knew that the work was not going to be easy.

I cannot say that I was very happy during those first months at Morton. I could not forget Mr Rochester. I repeated again and again that I had done right. I could not live with Mr Rochester while his first wife still lived.

Slowly, my work at the school began to have results. A number of my girls began to do their lessons well, and I was glad. I began to teach some of the older girls drawing and a little French. Their families were very happy.

St John Rivers came to the school twice a week to teach, and sometimes he visited my little house.

One evening in November he came to see me at home. I was painting a picture at the time, and he looked carefully at my work before he sat down. He stayed for about half an hour and then he stood up to leave. As he walked past my drawing, he stopped and looked at it again.

The next day there was a cold wind and the snow was very deep. It was quite late when I heard a knock at the door. I opened the door, and there was St John.

"Last night I discovered something strange," he said. "I've returned tonight so that you can explain it to me.

"About twenty years ago a clergyman fell in love with a rich man's daughter. Her family didn't want her to marry him, but she did. Two years later both she and her husband were dead. They left a daughter, who went to live with her rich uncle and aunt, Mr and Mrs Reed of Gateshead. I don't know whether this poor orphan was happy with her uncle's family, but when she was ten she was sent to Lowood School – you know the place because you were there yourself, weren't you? It's very strange – this orphan's story is very like yours. At the age of eighteen, this girl left Lowood. She went to work as a governess at a house called Thornfield Hall.

"Thornfield Hall belonged to a man called Rochester. I know very little about him, but I do know that he asked the girl to marry him. She agreed. But during the wedding, she discovered that he already had a wife.

"That night the governess left Thornfield Hall and no one has seen her since. Mr Rochester has searched everywhere, but she hasn't been found. I learned this from a lawyer in London, Mr Briggs. It's a strange, sad story, isn't it, Jane?"

"Tell me, St John – where is Mr Rochester now? How is he? Is he well? You must know about him. Please, please tell me," I begged.

"I'm afraid I don't know anything about Mr Rochester," St John answered. "But don't you want to know the name of the governess in the story? Briggs wrote to me about a Jane Eyre. I knew only a Jane Elliott. Jane Eyre is your real name, isn't it?"

"Yes, yes," I answered quickly. "Tell me, St John. Can I write to Mr Briggs? Do you think he'll be able to tell me more about Mr Rochester?"

"I don't think so, Jane. But forget Mr Rochester for a

moment and listen to me. Do you know why Mr Briggs wrote to me?"

"No," I answered.

"He wanted to tell me about your uncle, John Eyre of Madeira. He is dead, and you are now a rich woman."

"I? – Rich?" I cried.

"Yes, you – rich –very rich, in fact. Your uncle has left you twenty thousand pounds."

I was so surprised that I did not understand. Then I felt sad, because my uncle had been the only member of the family who cared about me.

"Why did Mr Briggs write to you?" I asked.

"Oh, I'm a clergyman, and clergymen are often asked about strange things," he answered.

"No," I replied. "Your answer isn't good enough. Mr Briggs didn't write to every clergyman in England, I'm sure."

"It's a very strange story, Jane," he said quietly. "Did you know that my name is St John Eyre Rivers?"

"No, I didn't," I said. And then suddenly I knew what had happened. But I said nothing, and St John continued.

"My mother's name was Eyre. She had two brothers. One was a clergyman, and he married Miss Jane Reed of Gateshead. The other was John Eyre of Madeira. Mr Briggs was John Eyre's lawyer, and he wrote to me last August. Do you remember? He told me that my uncle was dead. He also told me that my uncle had given his money to someone else. A few weeks ago I received another letter from Mr Briggs. He said that he could not find the woman who ought to have my uncle's money. Then last night I saw your name on that painting. By mistake you had signed it with your real name."

I said, "Let me try to understand. Your mother was my

father's sister. Is that right?"

"Yes."

"So she was my aunt?"

"Yes."

"So you, and Diana, and Mary are my cousins?"

I looked at him. It was wonderful! At last I had found some of my family. I felt very, very happy. I had been an orphan all my life. I had never known any kind of family love, and suddenly I had three cousins. More than that – they were three people I already knew and loved.

"Oh, St John," I cried. "I'm so happy – so happy!"

St John smiled. "Jane, you're the strangest girl I've ever known. When I told you that you were rich, you looked sad. Now, when I tell you that we're cousins, you're mad with happiness. I really don't understand you at all!"

"Perhaps you can't understand my happiness because you've never been completely alone in the world." Then I stopped – I was the person who had taken Uncle John's money from St John, Mary and Diana. I thought of a plan almost immediately. There were four cousins. If I kept all the money, I would be unhappy and my cousins would be poor. The answer was easy. If I divided the money, we would all have enough.

I told St John my thoughts. At first he did not like my plan. He thought that I would be sorry later. We talked for a long time. But in the end he agreed. He said that I must think carefully, but I could see that he was happy.

It was late when he left. "Well, Jane," he said, "the school? Must it close immediately?"

"No, no, of course not," I answered. "I'll continue until you find a new teacher."

He looked pleased. "Thank you," he said and smiled. "That will be a great help. And now, good night, cousin."

Chapter 16
Christmas

By Christmas everything had been done. The lawyer had divided my money equally between St John, Diana, Mary and me.

A week before Christmas, I closed the school for the holidays. When it opened again there would be a new teacher. I was strangely sad on my last day there. I knew I was leaving some very good friends. But I had other happinesses ahead of me. Diana and Mary were coming home at last. Now that they had money of their own, they did not need to work as governesses any more.

At last the great day came. St John came from Morton to meet his sisters.

Diana and Mary arrived at four o'clock in the afternoon. There was such excitement. I was so happy to see them again. They were tired after their long journey, but they were very glad to be home.

The week which followed was wonderful. We had a complete holiday. We spent many hours talking about the past and our plans for the future. St John did not often join our talk. I do not think he enjoyed the holiday. He thought that we were wasting our time.

One day, St John and I were alone in the sitting room. He was reading a book on Hindustani and I was learning German. He was learning Hindustani because he had decided to be a missionary in India. He asked me what I was doing.

"My German," I replied.

"I want you to stop German and learn Hindustani with me," he said.

"You aren't serious, are you?" I cried.

"Yes, Jane. I want you to help me. If I have to teach you the language, I'll also learn better myself," he said.

I did not really want to learn Hindustani but I could not say no. He was a good teacher, but I had to work very hard. Every time I did something well, he demanded something better. And I could not refuse.

During those winter months I did not forget Mr Rochester. I remembered him especially at night. At the time I began my Hindustani lessons with St John, I was waiting for a reply from Mr Briggs. I had written to him about Mr Rochester. At last I received a letter, but Mr Briggs could tell me nothing. Then I wrote to Mrs Fairfax, but she did not answer. I wrote again, but there was still no reply.

One morning in the early spring I felt very sad. St John and I were reading Hindustani together and suddenly I started to weep. I could not stop. St John waited for some minutes and then said, "Come for a walk with me, Jane,"

"I'll get Diana and Mary," I said.

"No," he answered. "Today we'll go alone."

The weather was beautiful. We walked up the hill behind the house.

"Shall we rest here?" St John asked when we reached some trees by a little river.

We sat down, and for some minutes we did not speak. Then St John said, "Jane, I'm leaving England in six weeks' time. My ship sails on 20th June. And you must come to India with me. Come and help me with my missionary work."

"Oh, St John, I can't," I cried.

"But you can, Jane. You'll be a very good missionary's wife. I've watched you carefully during these last months.

I know that you must be my wife."

"Give me time to think," I begged. "Please, leave me alone for a few minutes."

"Of course," he said, and he walked away along the river.

During the next quarter of an hour, I tried to think clearly. I knew that I could do the work. I was not a strong person, but I could do it. But St John had asked me to be his wife. My heart said no to this. I could not marry St John. He did not love me, and I did not love him. I had known real love, and I could not marry without it.

"Forgive me," I said. "I don't want to hurt you. Please, please forgive me, but I can never marry you. Please forget your plan."

That night after supper, in the darkness I heard a voice.

"Jane! Jane! Jane!" it cried.

"Oh, God – what is it?" I thought. But I knew already. It was the voice of Edward Rochester, the man I really loved.

"I'm coming! Wait for me!" I cried. "Where are you?"

Chapter 17
I look for Mr Rochester

The next morning I woke up before the sun rose. I dressed and packed a few things for my journey. I was going back to Thornfield. If letters could not tell me about Mr Rochester, I must find him myself.

At breakfast I told Mary and Diana that I had to go away. I said that I was worried about a friend. I thought that he needed me.

I left Moor House on Tuesday afternoon and I arrived at the George Hotel, Millcote, early on the following Thursday morning. I did not ask the man at the hotel about Thornfield. I wanted to see the place myself. I walked across the fields to the house – I wanted to be alone when I saw the house again.

At last I saw the tops of the trees which stood beside the house. I went closer. And then, when I saw the house, my heart stopped! It was no longer a house – it was only black stones! There were no windows, no roof – and grass was growing inside the high walls. There had been a great fire – and nothing remained. "What has happened? Where is Mr Rochester? Is he dead? And Adèle, Mrs Fairfax, all the servants – are they dead, too?"

I had to know the answers to these questions, and so I returned to Millcote. I went back to the George Hotel and asked for some breakfast. When the girl brought it, I asked her some questions.

"Do you know Thornfield Hall?" I asked.

"Yes, madam. I used to work there before Mr Rochester died," she replied.

"Is he dead?" I cried.

"I mean Mr Edward Rochester's father," she explained. I began to breathe more easily again.

"Is Mr Rochester at Thornfield Hall now?" I asked next.

"Oh, no, madam. You must be a stranger here, I think. There was a terrible fire at Thornfield Hall last autumn. It was late one night. Nothing was saved. I saw it myself."

"How did the fire start?" I continued.

"Well, madam, it's difficult to explain. Did you know that there was a mad woman at Thornfield?"

"Yes," I said. "I've heard something like that."

"Well – no one knew for certain who she was. But then, last year, a very strange thing happened. A governess came to work at the house. She taught the little French orphan who lived there. I never saw this governess. No one thought she was pretty, but Mr Rochester fell in love with her."

"Yes, yes," I said. "You can tell me that part of the story another time. At the moment I want to know about the fire. Did the mad woman start it?"

"Yes, she did. That's certain. She was a terrible woman and she sometimes escaped from her room on the third floor. A woman called Grace Poole looked after her. Grace was a good woman, but she had one big fault. She drank too much. And sometimes when she was drunk, the mad woman escaped. On the night of the fire, the mad woman went to the governess's room. She burned the bed and soon all of the house was on fire."

"Was Mr Rochester at home when the fire started?" I asked.

"Yes," the girl answered. "When the governess left, he went to look for her, but he never found her. He returned to Thornfield in the end. He behaved very bravely during the fire. He helped everyone to escape. Then he went upstairs to his mad wife. She was standing outside on the roof. Mr Rochester went towards her and shouted 'Bertha', but at that moment she jumped off the roof. She was dead when they picked her up."

"How terrible! What happened after that?"

"The house was completely burnt."

"Was anyone else killed?" I asked.

"No. But poor Mr Rochester ..." she stopped.

"Why – what happened? What do you mean?" I cried.

"Poor Mr Rochester." she said. "He's a different man now. He used to be so strong, but now ..."

"Where is he?" I cried. "Is he in England?"

"Yes, yes. He's in England. He can't travel now. He's blind, poor man. Blind. He can't see anything. The fire burnt both his eyes. People say that he'll never see again. He also lost one of his arms – his left one, I think."

I had feared worse.

"Where is he now?" I asked. "Where does he live?"

"At Ferndean Manor. It's about thirty miles from here. People say it's a very lonely place."

"Who is with him? Does anyone look after him?"

"Old John and his wife. They used to work at Thornfield Hall. Mr Rochester won't have anyone else. They're the only people with him."

"Have you got a carriage?" was my next question.

"Yes, madam. We have a very good one," she replied.

"Can I use it immediately? I must go to Ferndean at once."

Chapter 18
Together again!

Ferndean Manor was an old house. It was much older than Thornfield. It stood in the middle of a dark wood. It was not a beautiful or comfortable house. I left the carriage at the edge of the wood. I wanted to walk the last mile alone.

At last I came to some big gates. The girl at the George Hotel was right – it was a very lonely place. Inside the gates, a path led up to the front door of the house. As I stood by the gates, the front door opened. A man came out slowly. I knew who it was immediately. He had changed a lot, but it was certainly Mr Rochester. He moved very slowly and carefully. It began to rain and he lifted his eyes to the sky. But he could see nothing. He walked slowly back to the front door. I went around the house and knocked at another door. Mary, John's wife, opened it. She looked at me as if I were a ghost.

"Is it really you, Miss Eyre?" she asked. "What are you doing here so late in the evening?"

I sat down and tried to explain. I told Mary and John everything. Then I asked them if I could stay the night.

"Of course, Miss Eyre," Mary replied. "But I'm afraid you won't be very comfortable."

She was filling a glass of water when she said this. I took it from her, and said, "I'll take this to him. May I?"

She showed me the sitting room door and I went in. Pilot was lying in front of the fire. He jumped up when he saw me and was very excited. I put the water down on the table. Then I said, "Lie down, Pilot!"

Mr Rochester was sitting in a chair by the fire. He turned towards me.

Mr Rochester in his chair by the fire

"Give me the water, Mary," he said.

I gave it to him. Pilot was still excited.

"What's the matter?" Mr Rochester asked. "It is you, isn't it, Mary?"

"Mary's in the kitchen," I answered.

He put his hand out. He wanted to touch me. "Who is this? Who is this?" he asked quickly. "Answer me – speak again!" he cried.

"Pilot knows me. John and Mary know me," I said.

"Is it a ghost? Is it only a voice? Come here. I can't see you, but I can touch you." He put out his hand and I held it.

"It is her! These are her little fingers," he said quietly. Then he touched my face and hair. "Jane," he said gently. "It is my Jane, isn't it?"

"Yes, sir, it is. I'm back at last."

"Oh, my dearest Jane. You mustn't go away again. I shall die if you go. Will you marry me?"

"Yes, Edward, if you choose me. I'll follow your wishes," I said happily. I did not want him to be serious that evening. I wanted him to laugh a little. He had been sad for too long.

"But you don't want to marry an ugly, blind man like me, do you? And I *am* ugly now, aren't I?"

"Well, Edward, I never thought you were very good-looking. You know that!" And I laughed.

"But can you look at me?" he asked. "My left arm looks terrible, and I'm sure that my face must be frightening, too."

"Oh, no. I don't think so, Edward. Your hair is too long and wild at the moment. You look rather like a lion! But we can change that. No, I don't think you look strange or frightening at all. Now, I must put some wood on the fire.

Then we'll have supper."

"I never have supper," he said.

"Well, you must have some tonight. I'm very hungry and I don't want to eat alone."

And so he ate with me. We sat late over our meal. We were both completely happy. How different Mr Rochester and St John were! How glad I was to be with Mr Rochester again! He wanted to know everything I had done, but I refused to tell him that evening. It was too long for one evening, I said. I promised to tell him everything the next day.

I felt very sorry for him, but I knew that I must not let him know it. If I did, he would never be well again.

He was already there when I went down to the dining room for breakfast.

"It's a beautiful morning, Edward," I said happily. "The sun is shining again. Shall we go for a walk after breakfast?"

"So it wasn't a dream last night. Yes, we'll go for a walk and you must tell me about everything. From now on, Jane, you must be my eyes."

And so we spent most of the day in the open air. We walked a long way and we stopped to rest often. I told him about everything I saw. We were wonderfully happy. At last Edward sat down under a tree and took me on his knee.

"Now, Jane," he said. "I want to hear your story. Where have you been?"

I told him everything about the Rivers family. When I spoke of St John, I could see that Edward was jealous. I knew that this was a good thing, too! He was himself again.

"Shall we walk home through the wood?" I said at last.

As we walked he told me about something very

strange: "Listen – last Monday night I was very sad. I wanted you near, but I feared that you were dead. It was nearly midnight. I was sitting in my room. In my sadness I spoke three words, 'Jane – Jane – Jane'. Then I heard a voice, your voice, answer, 'I'm coming! Wait for me!' A moment later the same voice cried, 'Where are you?' I cannot explain it. I've thought about it a lot. But I'm sure that it was your voice. Isn't it strange?"

When I heard this story, I could not speak for a moment. I had heard Mr Rochester's voice at the same time. It was indeed very strange, but I did not tell Edward my story. There are some things which must not be said.

He held out his hand and I took it in mine. Slowly we walked home together. We had found happiness at last.

I married Mr Rochester. We had a quiet wedding. There were only the clergyman, his wife, Mr Rochester and I at the church. When we returned, I went to the kitchen. Mary and John were working there.

"Mr Rochester and I were married this morning," I told them.

Both Mary and John were honest, country people. They did not get excited easily. Mary looked up from her work and smiled.

"Well, Miss, I'm very pleased for you both," she said. And then she returned to her work.

John was smiling from ear to ear. "I knew it!" he cried. "I knew that Mr Rochester would marry you. And I'm very glad. I hope you'll both be very happy!"

I wrote to Moor House immediately. Diana and Mary were very happy. They come to visit us quite often. But St John did not write until six months later. He wrote only about his missionary work. We have continued to write to

Mr Rochester and Jane are married at last

each other once or twice a year since then. His letters are always very serious, but very kind.

I have not forgotten little Adèle, either. When we were married, she was away at school. I went to see her soon after the wedding. She was very excited when she saw me again, and I was very happy to see her, too. I could see that she was not happy at the school. It was a sad, serious place. I remembered Lowood as soon as I saw it. Adèle looked white and thin. I decided immediately that she must change schools. Edward agreed when I told him about her. And so she went to a school nearer Ferndean. She did well at the new school.

We see Mrs Fairfax at least once a year. Edward had given her a small house after the fire. And she has enough money to live comfortably near her friends.

My story is nearly finished. I have now been married for ten years. I know what happiness is at last. My husband's life and mine are the same life. We are very close. For the first two years, I had to do everything for him. During that time he was completely blind. And then slowly he began to see with one eye. One day he told me the colour of my dress. We went to London together soon after that, and Edward saw a famous doctor there. Now he can see quite well with one eye. I do not have to lead him everywhere. And when our first son was born he could see that the baby looked like him.

Questions

Questions on each chapter

1 1 Where did John Reed find Jane?
  2 What did he do to her?
  3 Why was Jane afraid of the red room?
  4 What did Dr Lloyd speak to Mrs Reed about?

2 1 Who was the very tall man in the sitting room?
  2 Who was Miss Temple?
  3 Who was Jane's special friend at Lowood?
  4 Where did Mr Brocklehurst make Jane stand?

3 1 Mr Brocklehurst did not go to the school in the spring.
   Why?
  2 Where did Helen say she was going?
  3 Who answered Jane's advertisement?

4 1 Who welcomed Jane at Thornfield Hall?
  2 Who was the owner of Thornfield Hall?
  3 What was the name of Jane's pupil?
  4 What was the frightening noise?

5 1 What happened to the horse on the icy road?
  2 How did Jane help the stranger?
  3 Who was the stranger?
  4 Where did Mr Rochester meet Adèle's mother?

6 1 Where did the smoke come from?
  2 Why was Mr Rochester wet?
  3 When Jane went back to her room, why couldn't she sleep?

7 1 Where did Mr Rochester go on the day after the fire?
  2 Who arrived on a horse, riding beside Mr Rochester?
  3 Why was Adèle excited?

8 1 Who went first to see the fortune teller?
  2 Who went last?
  3 Who was the fortune teller really?
  4 Who was the stranger, and where was his home?

9 1 What happened to Mason on the third floor?
  2 Who was the "young man" in Mr Rochester's story?
  3 Who was Mr Rochester's "new friend"?

10 1 Why did Jane go to Gateshead?
  2 Who had written to Mrs Reed?
  3 What did Mrs Reed tell him about Jane Eyre?

11 1 Why did Miss Ingram stop speaking to Mr Rochester?
  2 What was Mrs Fairfax's advice to Jane?
  3 Who did Jane write to?
  4 What was the tall woman's face like?

12 1 Who stopped the wedding in the church?
  2 What reason did he give?
  3 Who was the animal-like woman on the third floor?
  4 Who had asked Mr Mason to stop the wedding?

13 1 Why did Mr Rochester's father want his son to marry
    Bertha Mason?
  2 What did Mr Rochester discover about his wife's mother?
  3 What was Grace Poole's work?

14 1 How much money did Jane have?
  2 What did the people in the village give to Jane?
  3 Who gave Jane some bread?
  4 What did Jane say her name was?

15 1 What work did St John offer Jane?
  2 St John received a letter. What did it tell them?
  3 Who told St John the facts about Jane Eyre?
  4 Jane was now "a rich woman". How did that happen?
  5 What did she decide to do with the money?

16 1 Why was St John learning Hindustani?
  2 What did St John ask Jane to become?
  3 What did Jane hear in the darkness?
  4 What did Jane answer?

17 1 What happened to Thornfield Hall?
   2 Who died?
   3 What happened to Mr Rochester?

18 1 What did Jane take to the sitting room?
   2 What did Pilot do?
   3 What had Edward heard on Monday night?
   4 Why did Jane find another school for Adèle?
   5 What happened to Edward's eyesight after two years?

Questions on the whole story

These are harder questions. Read the Introduction, and think hard about the questions before you answer them. Some of them ask for your opinion, and there is no fixed answer.

1 Are there still schools like Lowood anywhere in the world?

2 Why do you think Mr Brocklehurst was so cruel?

3 What do you think of Edward Rochester?
   a What effect had his early life had on his character?
   b Why did Jane love him?
   c What excuse can you find for his deceiving her?
   d How did he behave at the time of the Thornfield fire?
   e Are you glad that he finds happiness in the end? Why?

4 St John Rivers:
   a How did he help Jane?
   b Why did he want to marry Jane?
   c Where did he go in the end?

5 Jane Eyre:
   a How did her early life affect her character?
   b Can you find examples of her independence of mind?
   c What did Edward Rochester find lovable in her?
   d Why did she refuse to marry St John Rivers?
   e Do you think the ending of the story is right for her? Can you give some reasons?

6 Do you find it hard to believe any of the situations or happenings in the story? Why?

7 What was Charlotte Brontë's main purpose in writing this story?

New words

clergyman
a priest of an English church

coach
a large enclosed four-wheeled horse-drawn carriage

governess
a woman teacher who lived in a family and educated the children at home

lonely
feeling that you are alone, wanting to have friends but not having them

missionary
a person who is sent, usually to a foreign country, to teach and spread his or her religion there

novel
a long story with invented people and happenings, printed as a book

orphan
a child who has no parents

publish
print and sell books

typhus
a serious and dangerous disease with high fever

West Indies
a group of islands in the Caribbean Sea